The Worry Worm

Story By Lazer Brody

Written & Illustrated By Rebecca Shapiro

Little Lazer

For Growing Kids...
With Growing Minds

Printed in USA

Published by

Inspiring Ink Press
12555 Biscayne Boulevard, Suite 400
Miami, FL 33181

ISBN 978-0-9829740-1-8

Many wonderful people were instrumental in bringing "The Worry Worm" to press. First and foremost, I'd like to thank The Almighty for enabling me to devote my life to spreading the message of hope and faith among people from around the globe.

Without Rebecca Shapiro's superb talents and indescribable dedication, this book could have never seen the light of day. Her wonderful husband Avi selflessly enabled her to devote whatever time she needed to complete this project. May they both be blessed with all their heart's wishes for the very best.

The "Rocket Team" – David Reckles, Michael Sigel, and Cynthia Nelson – has now made my books and CDs readily available everywhere. May The Almighty bless them and their families with all their hearts' wishes for the very best.

A special thank you to our junior editors – the Shapiro children; Moshe Tzvi, Mordechai Duniel & Yonah Pesach, who listened to their mother read the book over and over, and gave invaluable feedback, giving their opinions of every illustration.

A warm note of thanks goes to Alissa Klapman and to Joy Zians for their valuable input.

My wife Yehudit, may The Almighty bless her always, deserves the credit for everything I do. What's mine is hers.

Lazer Brody
September 2010

One beautiful bright sunny day in the fall,
The apples were swaying and the trees looked so tall.
Farmer Fred's apple farm is the place to be.
There is so much to do there, and so much to see.
Robbie, the nephew of old Farmer Fred,
would go there to fill up the brains in his head.

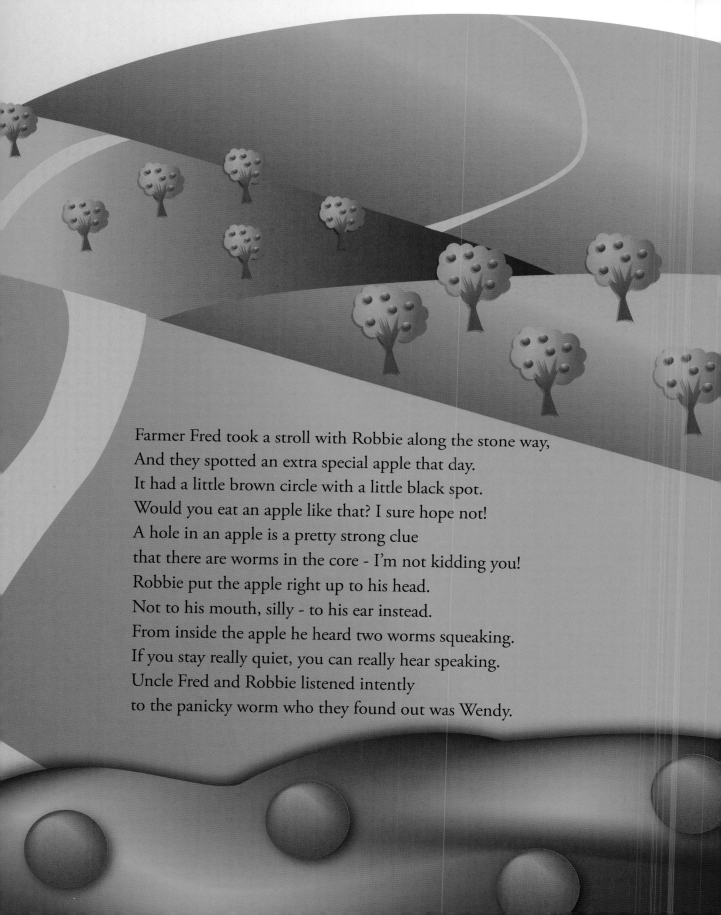

Farmer Fred took a stroll with Robbie along the stone way,
And they spotted an extra special apple that day.
It had a little brown circle with a little black spot.
Would you eat an apple like that? I sure hope not!
A hole in an apple is a pretty strong clue
that there are worms in the core - I'm not kidding you!
Robbie put the apple right up to his head.
Not to his mouth, silly - to his ear instead.
From inside the apple he heard two worms squeaking.
If you stay really quiet, you can really hear speaking.
Uncle Fred and Robbie listened intently
to the panicky worm who they found out was Wendy.

"The end of the world is near! I've had it! I'm through!
It's cold and it's dark, and there's nothing to do.
This rumbling and shaking is driving me crazy!
I'm scared and I'm freezing and everything's hazy!"

"Wendy, don't be silly," her worm sister replied,
"I'm right over here, I'm right by your side.
There's no need to worry, there's no need to fear,
If you'll simply lend me your ear.
It's me, Wilma – your sister and friend.
This apple is not our life – it's our means to an end."

"Wilma honey, you have a few loose screws in your brain.
What is an apple? You sound so insane!"

Wilma had to think about something fast
To teach her sister about the world that is vast.
"Wendy, you must stop being so mean.
I know it's hard to imagine something you've never seen.
We were born in this apple two weeks ago
And before Mother left, she taught me all we need to know.
All about life when we leave our apple home,
About endless leaves to eat, and fun places we will roam."

Wendy interrupted. I bet that's no surprise.
"You're crazier than I thought – you're not so wise.".
Making up stories about a mother and food,
Your fairy tales are ruining my mood.
It's shaky and dark – what other proof do you need?
The world is ending at a rapid speed!"

Now Wendy there's something you really must know
Worry is not helping so please end this drama show.
This is the truth – lying is something I never do.
Close your eyes and imagine what I'm saying to you.
(Yes, you out there listening, you can do it too!)

We were born in an apple on a bright sunny day.
The wind blew gently, making us sway.
When picked from the tree we felt a big shock
And the shakes after that… I know you have a mental block…
But there's something called humans – they picked our apple from the tree.
That's why we are shaking - just wait & see!

Worms pass down this knowledge from one to the other.
A most valuable lesson to keep in mind,
Is the One who created us never leaves anyone behind.
He's always behind all the good and the (seemingly) bad
He takes care of our needs, He's our loving Dad.
Not the one who is married to our mother,
The one all around us – we can't see him, but we know there's no other.

And I know what I know because I'm a smart worm
And on this point I'll stay incredibly firm.
No worry is needed, when we continue to trust,
For smart little worms, trust is a must!

"Wilma, you are so full of baloney!
Either you're sorely mis-informed or a really big phony!
My ignorant sister, you need some serious help!
Our lives are in danger, and there's no way out —Yelp!"

Uncle Fred decided to aid Wilma's (almost) helpless cause.
He put the apple on the ground without any pause,
And carefully cut out a piece from one side.
Wilma & Wendy popped their heads out — eyes open wide!

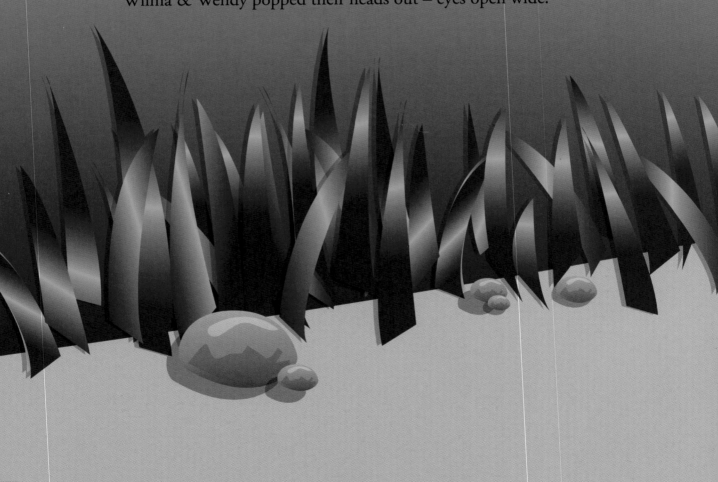

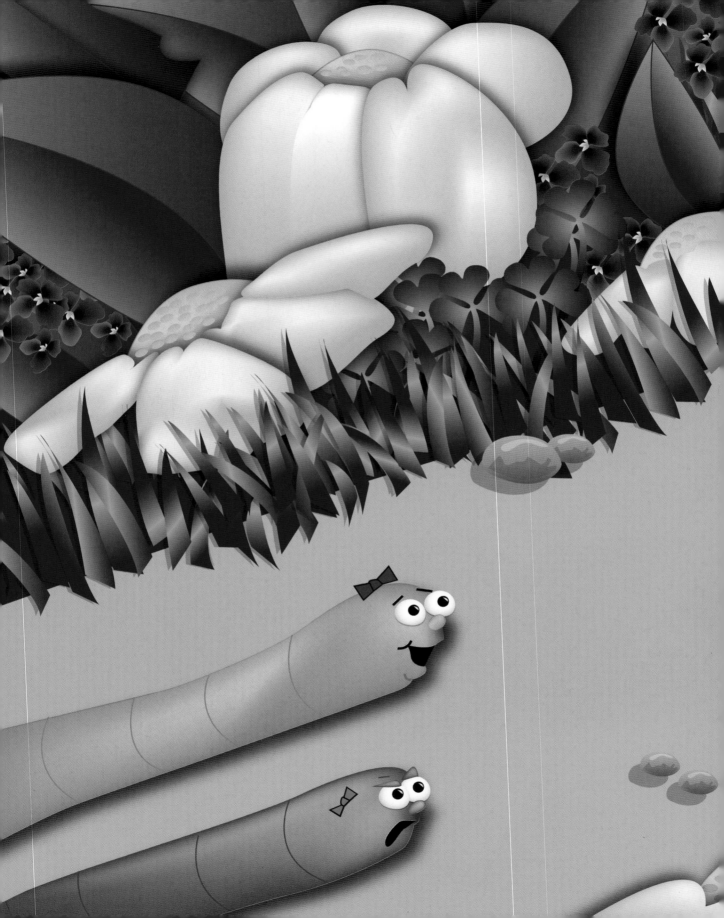

"See, look Wendy dear, it's just as I said.
It's incredible out here – oh, look up ahead!
There are clovers and mint and sweet-smelling flowers!
Oh boy, I can't wait to explore for hours!"

"Oh no, crazy sister, this is worse than before!
We're dead, it's all over – that, you cannot ignore.
Our lives as we know it are completely over -
no matter what you say about mint and clover."

"So you think we're dead – huh? I'll show you stubborn sister,"
and Wilma turned to Wendy and lovingly bit her.

"Ouch, that wasn't nice! What was that for?
I know I annoyed you a little before
But if it hurt, I guess I'm not dead
Maybe there's a different explanation instead."

"Wendy I'm happy you're starting to comprehend
Our lives are just beginning – they are not at an end!
You wasted a whole day with worry and rage
When we could have been on the same page.
If we trust in our Creator to fulfill every need,
Then there's no need for worry, for anger or greed.
He personally cares for every creation
Whether it's a worm, a person, or an entire nation.

And I know what I know because I'm a smart worm
And on this point I'll stay incredibly firm.
No worry is needed, when we continue to trust,
For smart little worms, trust is a must!

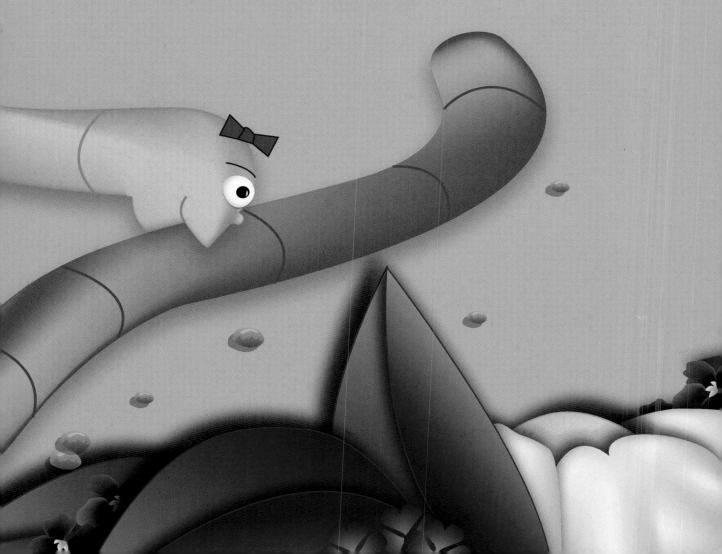

"I think I'm starting to understand your position.
I'm sorry it took me all day to transition."
Wendy felt sorry she was mean the whole day.
"I'd like to make it up to you, Wilma. Just tell me the way"

"Don't worry dear sister, I'm just happy we're through,
staying happy and calm is the best thing to do.
There's no need to worry about anything,
Think how our Creator, our Father, our King,
protects us and loves us through thick and thin
with that in mind – you will always win!
So even though we might not understand,
When we trust Him, life becomes grand!

And I know what I know because I'm a smart worm
And on this point I'll stay incredibly firm.
No worry is needed, when we continue to trust,
For smart little worms, trust is a must!

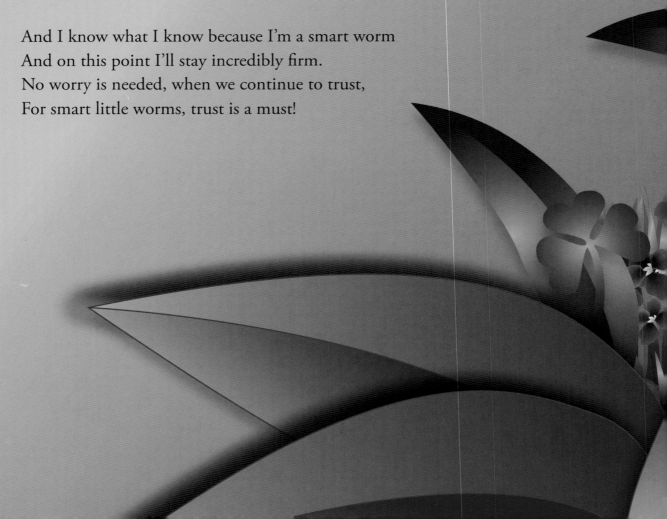

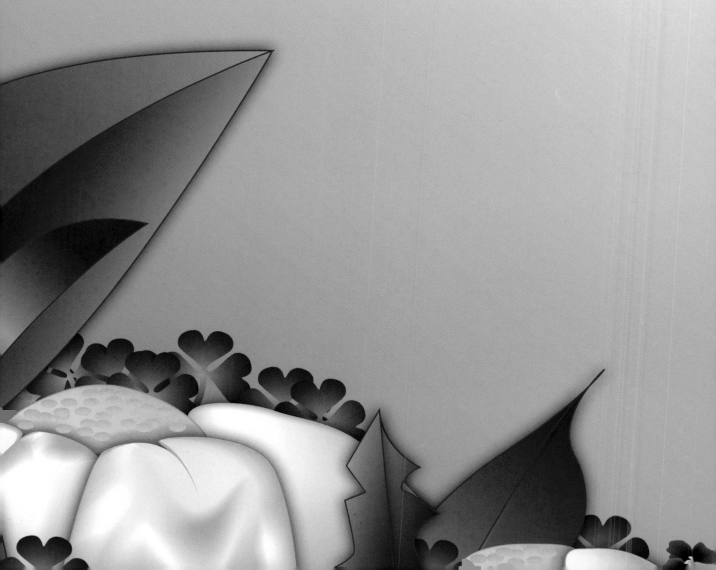

Uncle Fred and Robbie looked at each other with a smile.
It's incredible what you learn when you listen for awhile
To a pair of two worms on a warm sunny day -
For this kind of lesson – there's no money to pay!
Wilma & Wendy taught Robbie & Fred
an important lesson to keep in your head.

If the smartest of worms know how to trust,
Then the smartest of humans certainly must!